Uh-oh!
Chicken pox!

Under my shirt.
Under my socks.

Itchy, itchy
chicken pox.

Don't rub.
Don't scratch.

8

Oh, no!
Another batch!

9

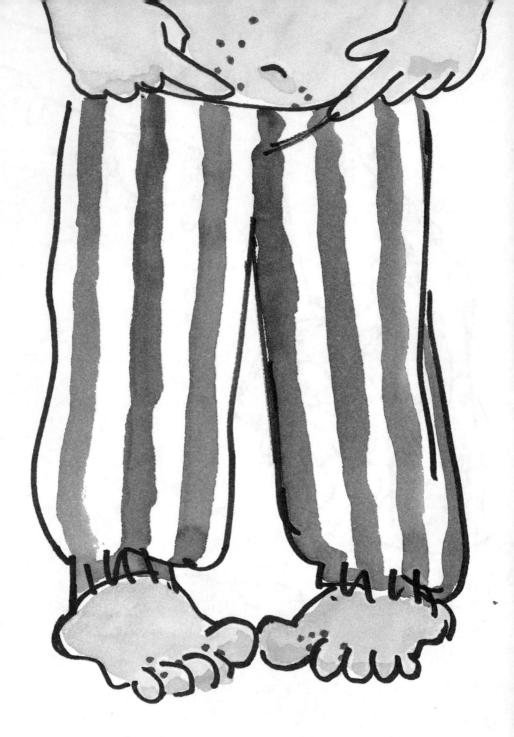

On my tummy,
between my toes,

down my back,
on my nose!

Lotion on.
Itching's gone
just for now.

It comes back—
OW!

One and two
and three and four.
Five and six...
and more and more.

Daddy counts
my itchy spots.
Lots and lots
of chicken pox.

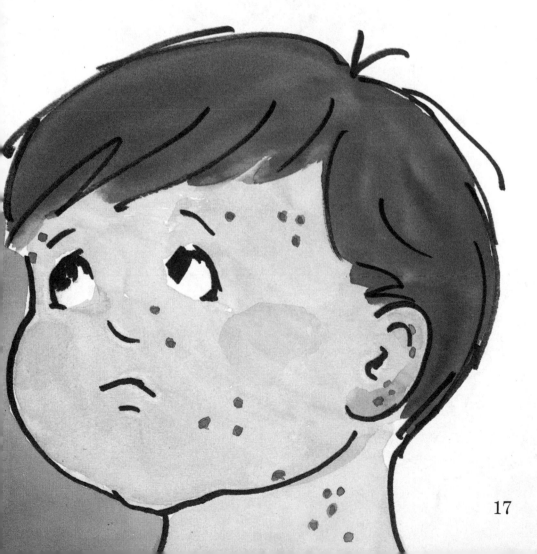

Itchy, itchy,
I feel twitchy....

I run away.
The itching stays.

Rubber ducky doesn't
like my yucky, mucky
oatmeal bath.
But Mommy says
it's good for me.

I rest.

I read.

STORY
BOOK

I eat.

I play.

25

I feel better
every day.

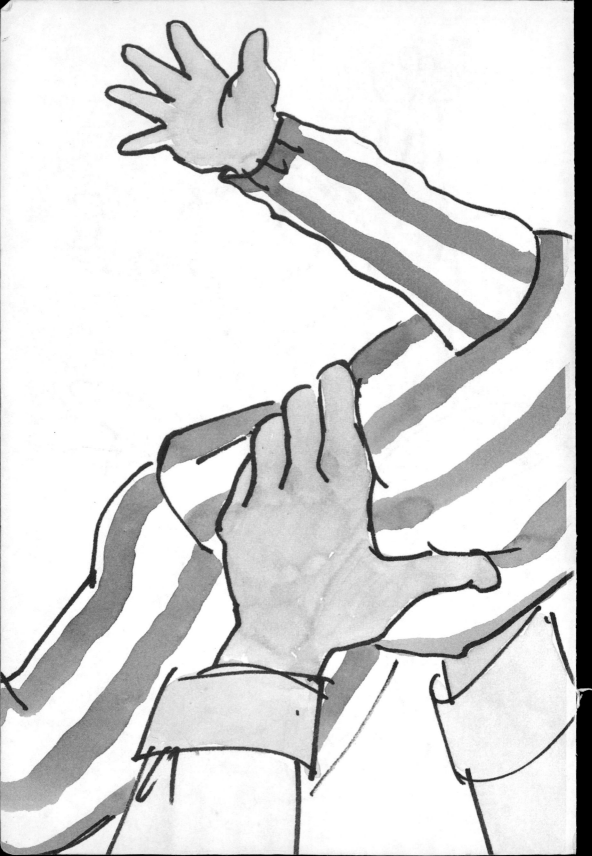

And then...
no new spots.
Hooray!

I'm okay!
I get to go
to school today!